Mother Goose

Frank Baber's

MoTher Goose

Nursery Rhymes

Selected by Ruth Spriggs

Illustrated by Frank Baber

Peter Lowe

THE ARTIST
Frank Baber was born in Bolton, Lancashire
and received his training at the Bolton
College of Art. He has spent all his working
life (apart from war service) as a practising
artist, working in such varied fields as
advertising illustration, textile design, the
theatre, architecture, portrait painting and
book illustration. His pictures have been
exhibited by the Royal Society of Portrait
Painters, the Royal Society of British
Artists and the Manchester Academy. He
has four children and three grandchildren.

ISBN 0 85654 021 8

Phototypeset by Tradespools Ltd, Frome, Somerset
Printed in Italy by New Interlitho SpA, Milan.

8

Old Mother Goose,
When she wanted to wander,
Would ride through the air
On a very fine gander.

She lived in a house
That was built in a wood
Where an owl at the door
For a sentinel stood.

She had a son, Jack,
A plain-looking lad;
He was not very good,
Nor yet very bad.

She sent him to market,
A live goose he bought.
"Here, Mother," says he,
"It will not go for naught."

Jack's goose and her gander
Grew very fond;
They'd both eat together,
Or swim in the pond.

Jack found one morning,
As I have been told,
His goose had laid for him
An egg of pure gold.

Jack ran to his mother,
The news for to tell.
She called him a good boy
And said it was well.

Jack sold his gold egg
To a rascally knave,
Not half of its value
To poor Jack he gave.

Then Jack went a-courting
A lady so gay,
As fair as a lily,
And sweet as the may.

The knave and the squire
Came up at his back,
And began to belabour
The sides of poor Jack.

But old Mother Goose
That instant came in,
And turned her son Jack
Into famed Harlequin.

She then with her wand
Touched the lady so fine,
And turned her at once
Into sweet Columbine.

And then the gold egg
Was thrown into the sea,
When Jack he jumped in
And got it again.

The knave got the goose,
Which he vowed he would kill,
Resolving at once
His pockets to fill.

But old Mother Goose
The goose saddled soon,
And mounting its back,
Flew up to the moon.

Hannah Bantry, in the pantry,
Gnawing at a mutton bone;
 How she gnawed it,
 How she clawed it,
When she found herself alone.

"What's in the cupboard?"
 Says Mr. Hubbard.
"A knuckle of veal,"
 Says Mr. Beal.
"Is that all?"
 Says Mr. Ball.
"And enough too,"
 Says Mr. Glue;
And away they all flew.

Pease porridge hot,
Pease porridge cold,
Pease porridge in the pot
Nine days old.

Some like it hot,
Some like it cold,
Some like it in the pot,
Nine days old.

Little Tommy Tucker,
 Sings for his supper:
What shall we give him?
 White bread and butter.
How shall he cut it
 Without a knife?
How will he be married
 Without a wife?

The greedy man is he who sits
 And bites bits out of plates,
Or else takes up an almanac
 And gobbles all the dates.

A little old man of Derby,
How do you think he served me?
He took away my bread and cheese,
And that is how he served me.

Davy, Davy Dumpling,
 Boil him in a pot!
Sugar him and butter him,
 And eat him while he's hot.

Jack Sprat could eat no fat,
 His wife could eat no lean,
And so between them both, you see,
 They licked the platter clean.

Wine and cake for gentlemen,
Hay and corn for horses,
A cup of ale for good old wives,
And kisses for young lasses.

Little fishes in a brook,
Father caught them on a hook,
Mother fried them in a pan,
Johnny eats them like a man.

Dance to your daddy,
My little babby,
Dance to your daddy, my little lamb;
You shall have a fishy
In a little dishy,
You shall have a fishy when the boat comes in.

Round and round the garden,
Like a teddy bear,
One step, two step,
Tickle you under there!

Clap hands, clap hands,
Till father comes home;
For father's got money,
But mother's got none.

Brow bender,
Eye peeper,
Nose dreeper,
Mouth eater,
Chin chopper,
Knock at the door,
Ring the bell,
Lift the latch,
Walk in . . .
Take a chair,
Sit by there,
How d'you do this morning?

Hush-a-bye baby,
Daddy is near,
Mammy's a lady
And that's very clear.

Hush, little baby, don't say a word,
Papa's going to buy you a mocking bird.

Pat-a-cake, pat-a-cake, baker's man,
Bake me a cake as fast as you can;
Pat it and prick it, and mark it with B,
And put it in the oven for baby and me.

If the mocking bird won't sing,
Papa's going to buy you a diamond ring.

If the diamond ring turns to brass,
Papa's going to buy you a looking-glass.

If the looking-glass gets broke,
Papa's going to buy you a billy-goat.

If that billy goat runs away
Papa's going to buy you another today.

How many days has my baby to play?
Saturday, Sunday, Monday,
Tuesday, Wednesday, Thursday, Friday,
Saturday, Sunday, Monday.
Hop away, skip away,
My baby wants to play,
My baby wants to play every day.

Ride a cock-horse to Banbury Cross,
To see a fine lady upon a white horse;
Rings on her fingers and bells on her toes,
And she shall have music wherever she goes.

Of all the gay birds that e'er I did see,
The owl is the fairest by far to me,
For all day long she sits on a tree,
And when night comes away flies she.

Little Robin Redbreast
Sat upon a rail;
Niddle noddle went his head,
Wiggle waggle went his tail.

Hickety, pickety, my black hen,
She lays eggs for gentlemen;
Gentlemen come every day
To see what my black hen doth lay.
Sometimes nine and sometimes ten,
Hickety, pickety, my black hen.

Two little dicky birds,
Sitting on a wall;
One named Peter,
The other named Paul.

Fly away, Peter!
Fly away, Paul!
Come back, Peter!
Come back, Paul!

Little Poll Parrot
Sat in his garret
Eating toast and tea;
A little brown mouse
Jumped into the house,
And stole it all away.

The cock crows in the morn
To tell us to rise,
And he that lies late
Will never be wise:
For early to bed,
And early to rise,
Makes a man healthy
And wealthy and wise.

Swan swam over the sea,
Swim, swan, swim!
Swan swam back again,
Well swum swan!

Once I saw a little bird
  Come hop, hop, hop,
And I cried, "Little bird,
  Will you stop, stop, stop?"

I was going to the window,
  To say, "How do you do?"
But he shook his little tail
  And away he flew.

A wise old owl lived in an oak;
The more he saw the less he spoke;
The less he spoke the more he heard.
Why can't we all be like that wise old bird?

Grey goose and gander,
  Waft your wings together,
And carry the good king's daughter
  Over the one-strand river.

The north wind doth blow,
And we shall have snow,
And what will poor robin do then,
  Poor thing?
He'll sit in a barn,
And keep himself warm,
And hide his head under his wing,
  Poor thing.

I had two pigeons bright and gay,
They flew from me the other day;
What was the reason they did go?
I cannot tell, for I do not know.

There was an owl lived in an oak,
  Wisky, wasky, weedle;
And every word he ever spoke
  Was "Fiddle, faddle, feedle."

A gunner chanced to come that way,
  Wisky, wasky, weedle;
Says he, "I'll shoot you silly bird."
  Fiddle, faddle, feedle.

17

Three young rats with black felt hats,
Three young ducks with white straw flats,
Three young dogs with curling tails,
Three young cats with demi-veils,
Went out to walk with two young pigs
In satin vests and sorrel wigs.
But suddenly it chanced to rain
And so they all went home again.

Now what do you think
    Of little Jack Jingle?
Before he was married,
    He used to live single.

But after he married,
    To alter his life,
He left off living single,
    And lived with his wife.

Bobby Shafto's gone to sea,
    Silver buckles at his knee;
He'll come back and marry me,
    Bonny Bobby Shafto!

Bobby Shafto's fat and fair,
    Combing down his yellow hair;
He's my love for evermore,
    Bonny Bobby Shafto!

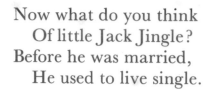
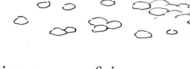

One, two, three, four,
Mary at the cottage door,
Five, six, seven, eight,
Eating cherries off a plate.

Little Tommy Tittlemouse
Lived in a little house;
He caught fishes
In other men's ditches.

Sing a song of sixpence,
    A pocket full of rye;
Four and twenty blackbirds,
    Baked in a pie.

When the pie was opened,
    The birds began to sing;
Wasn't that a dainty dish,
    To set before the king?

I had a little moppet,
I kept it in my pocket
And fed it on corn and hay;
Then came a proud beggar
And said he would wed her,
And stole my little moppet away.

The king was in his counting-house,
    Counting out his money;
The queen was in the parlour,
    Eating bread and honey.

The maid was in the garden,
    Hanging out the clothes,
When down came a blackbird,
    And snapped off her nose.

There was a man and he had nought,
    And robbers came to rob him;
He crept up to the chimney top,
    And then they thought they had him.

And he got down on the other side,
    And then they could not find him;
He ran fourteen miles in fifteen days,
    And never looked behind him.

One I love, two I love,
    Three I love, I say,
Four I love with all my heart,
    Five I cast away;
Six he loves, seven she loves, eight both love.
    Nine he comes, ten he tarries,
Eleven he courts, twelve he marries.

Oh dear, what can the matter be?
Dear, dear, what can the matter be?
Oh dear, what can the matter be?
Johnny's so long at the fair.

He promised he'd buy me a fairing should please me,
And then for a kiss, oh! he vowed he would tease me,
He promised he'd bring me a bunch of blue ribbons
To tie up my bonny brown hair.

He promised he'd bring me a basket of posies,
A garland of lilies, a garland of roses,
A little straw hat, to set off the blue ribbons
That tie up my bonny brown hair.

"Old woman, old woman, shall we go a-shearing?"
"Speak a little louder, sir, I'm very hard of hearing."
"Old woman, old woman, shall I love you dearly?"
"Thank you very kindly, sir, now I hear you clearly."

The barber shaved the mason,
    As I suppose,
    Cut off his nose,
And popped it in a basin.

Anna Maria she sat on the fire;
The fire was too hot, she sat on the pot;
The pot was too round, she sat on the ground;
The ground was too flat, she sat on the cat;
The cat ran away with Maria on her back.

Curly locks, Curly locks,
    Wilt thou be mine?
Thou shalt not wash dishes
    Nor yet feed the swine,
But sit on a cushion
    And sew a fine seam,
And feed upon strawberries,
    Sugar and cream.

Ickle, ockle, blue bockle,
Fishes in the sea,
If you want a pretty maid,
Please choose me.

Polly put the kettle on,
Polly put the kettle on,
Polly put the kettle on,
    We'll all have tea.

Sukey take it off again,
Sukey take it off again,
Sukey take it off again,
    They've all gone away.

Old chairs to mend! Old chairs to mend!
I never would cry old chairs to mend,
If I'd as much money as I could spend,
I never would cry old chairs to mend.

Old clothes to sell! Old clothes to sell!
I never would cry old clothes to sell,
If I'd as much money as I could tell,
I never would cry old clothes to sell.

When I was a little boy I lived by myself,
And all the bread and cheese I got I laid upon a shelf;
The rats and the mice they made such a strife,
I had to go to London town to buy me a wife.

The streets were so broad and the lanes were so narrow,
I was forced to bring my wife home in a wheelbarrow,
The wheelbarrow broke and my wife had a fall,
Farewell wheelbarrow, little wife and all.

As I was going to St. Ives,
I met a man with seven wives,
Each wife had seven sacks,
Each sack had seven cats,
Each cat had seven kits:
Kits, cats, sacks and wives,
How many were there going to St. Ives?

There was a rat, for want of stairs,
Went down a rope to say his prayers.

If wishes were horses,
Beggars would ride;
If turnips were watches
I would wear one by my side.

The girl in the lane, that couldn't speak plain,
    Cried, Gobble, gobble, gobble.
The man on the hill, that couldn't stand still,
    Went hobble, hobble, hobble.

Penny and penny
Laid up will be many;
Who will not save a penny
Shall never have any.

Old Mother Shuttle
Lived in a coal-scuttle
Along with her dog and her cat;
What they ate I can't tell,
But 'tis known very well
That not one of the party was fat.

Old Mother Shuttle
Scoured out her coal-scuttle,
And washed both her dog and her cat;
The cat scratched her nose,
So they came to hard blows,
And who was the gainer by that?

Humpty Dumpty sat on a wall,
Humpty Dumpty had a great fall,
  All the king's horses,
  And all the king's men,
Couldn't put Humpty together again.

Solomon Grundy
Born on a Monday,
Christened on Tuesday,
Married on Wednesday,
Took ill on Thursday,
Worse on Friday,
Died on Saturday,
Buried on Sunday,
This is the end
Of Solomon Grundy.

Hector Protector was dressed all in green;
Hector Protector was sent to the Queen.
The Queen did not like him,
No more did the King;
So Hector Protector was sent back again.

I had a little dog and they called him Buff,
I sent him to a shop to buy me snuff,
But he lost the bag and spilled the stuff;
I sent him no more but gave him a cuff,
For coming from the market without any snuff.

There was a bee
  Sat on a wall,
And "Buzz" said he,
  And that was all.

There was a crooked man, and he walked a crooked mile,
He found a crooked sixpence against a crooked stile;
He bought a crooked cat, which caught a crooked mouse,
And they all lived together in a little crooked house.

Blow, wind, blow! and go, mill go!
That the miller may grind his corn;
  That the baker may take it,
  And into bread make it,
And bring us a loaf in the morn.

26

Tom tied a kettle to the tail of a cat;
Jill put a stone in the blind man's hat;
Bob threw his grandmother down the stairs—
And they all grew up ugly and nobody cares.

Molly, my sister, and I fell out,
And what do you think it was all about?
She loved coffee and I lived tea,
And that was the reason we could not agree.

William and Mary, George and Anne,
Four such children had never a man;
They put their father to flight and shame,
And called their brother a shocking bad name.

There was a little girl, and she had a little curl
Right in the middle of her forehead;
When she was good, she was very, very good,
But when she was bad, she was horrid.

Tell tale tit!
Your tongue shall be slit,
And all the dogs in the town
Shall have a little bit.

Here's Sulky Sue;
What shall we do?
Turn her face to the wall
Till she comes to.

Multiplication is vexation,
Division is as bad;
The rule of three perplexes me,
And practice drives me mad.

Mary, Mary, quite contrary,
  How does your garden grow?
With silver bells and cockle shells,
  And pretty maids all in a row.

Tweedledum and Tweedledee
  Agreed to have a battle,
For Tweedledum said Tweedledee
  Had spoiled his nice new rattle.
Just then flew by a monstrous crow,
  As big as a tar-barrel,
Which frightened both the heroes so,
  They quite forgot their quarrel.

Don't care didn't care,
  Don't care was wild;
Don't care stole plum and pear
  Like any beggar's child.

Don't care was made to care,
  Don't care was hung;
Don't care was put in a pot
  And boiled till he was done.

Cry baby, cry,
Put your finger in your eye,
And tell your mother it wasn't I.

When Jacky's a good boy,
  He shall have cakes and custard;
But when he does nothing but cry,
  He shall have nothing but mustard.

Punch and Judy
  Fought for a pie;
Punch gave Judy
  A knock in the eye.
Says Punch to Judy
  "Will you have any more?"
Says Judy to Punch,
  "My eye is sore."

Cross-patch,
  Draw the latch,
Sit by the fire and spin;
  Take a cup,
  And drink it up,
Then call your neighbours in.

Georgie Porgie, pudding and pie,
Kissed the girls and made them cry;
When the boys came out to play,
Georgie Porgie ran away.

I do not like thee, Doctor Fell,
The reason why I cannot tell;
But this I know, and know full well,
I do not like thee, Doctor Fell.

Robin the Bobbin, the big-bellied Ben,
He ate more meat than fourscore men;
He ate a cow, he ate a calf,
He ate a butcher and a half,
He ate a church, he ate a steeple,
He ate the priest and all the people!
A cow and a calf,
An ox and a half,
A church and a steeple,
And all the good people,
And yet he complained that his stomach
wasn't full.

"Where are you going to, my pretty maid?"
"I'm going a-milking, sir," she said.

"May I go with you, my pretty maid?"
"You're kindly welcome, sir," she said.

"Say, will you marry me, my pretty maid?"
"Yes, if you please, kind sir," she said.

"What is your father, my pretty maid?"
"My father's a farmer, sir," she said.

"What is your fortune, my pretty maid?"
"My face is my fortune, sir," she said.

"Then I can't marry you, my pretty maid."
"Nobody asked you, sir," she said.

My maid Mary
She minds her dairy,
While I go a-hoeing and mowing each morn;
Merrily run the reel,
And the little spinning-wheel,
Whilst I am singing and mowing my corn.

The cock's on the wood pile a-blowing his horn,
The bull's in the barn, a-threshing of corn,
The maids in the meadows are making of hay,
The ducks in the river are swimming away.

Three blind mice, see how they run!
They all ran after the farmer's wife,
Who cut off their tails with a carving knife,
Did ever you see such a thing in your life,
        As three blind mice?

Cushy cow, bonny, let down thy milk,
And I will give thee a gown of silk;
A gown of silk and a silver tee,
If thou wilt let down thy milk to me.

Diddlety, diddlety, dumpty,
The cat ran up the plum tree;
    Half a crown
    To fetch her down,
Diddlety, diddlety, dumpty.

Chook, chook, chook, chook, chook,
"Good Morning, Mrs. Hen.
How many chicks have you got?"
"Madam, I've got ten.
Four of them are yellow,
And four of them are brown,
The nicest in the town."
Chook, chook, chook, chook, chook,
Cock-a-doodle-doo.

"Baa, baa, black sheep,
    Have you any wool?"
"Yes, sir, yes, sir,
    Three bags full;
    One for the master,
    And one for the dame,
And one for the little boy
    Who lives down the lane."

Donkey, donkey, old and grey,
Open your mouth and gently bray;
Lift your ears and blow your horn,
To wake the world this sleepy morn.

"Willy boy, Willy boy, where are you going?
    I will go with you, if that I may."
"I'm going to the meadow to see them a-mowing,
    I'm going to help them to make the new hay."

Young lambs to sell! Young lambs to sell!
I never would cry young lambs to sell,
If I'd as much money as I could tell,
I never would cry young lambs to sell.

Higglety, pigglety, pop!
The dog has eaten the mop!
    The pig's in a hurry,
    The cat's in a flurry,
Higglety, pigglety, pop!

Bell horses, bell horses,
    What time of day?
One o'clock, two o'clock,
    Time to away.

33

The lion and the unicorn
    Were fighting for the crown;
The lion beat the unicorn
    All round about the town.

Some gave them white bread,
    And some gave them brown;
Some gave them plum cake
    And drummed them out of town.

London Bridge is falling down,
  Falling down, falling down,
London Bridge is falling down,
  My fair lady.

Build it up with wood and clay,
  Wood and clay, wood and clay,
Build it up with wood and clay,
  My fair lady.

Wood and clay will wash away,
  Wash away, wash away,
Wood and clay will wash away,
  My fair lady.

Build it up with bricks and mortar,
  Bricks and mortar, bricks and mortar,
Build it up with bricks and mortar,
  My fair lady.

Bricks and mortar will not stay,
  Will not stay, will not stay,
Bricks and mortar will not stay,
  My fair lady.

Build it up with iron and steel,
  Iron and steel, iron and steel,
Build it up with iron and steel,
  My fair lady.

Iron and steel will bend and bow,
  Bend and bow, bend and bow,
Iron and steel will bend and bow,
  My fair lady.

Build it up with silver and gold,
  Silver and gold, silver and gold,
Build it up with silver and gold,
  My fair lady.

Silver and gold will be stolen away,
  Stolen away, stolen away,
Silver and gold will be stolen away,
  My fair lady.

Set a man to watch all night,
  Watch all night, watch all night.
Set a man to watch all night,
  My fair lady.

Suppose the man should fall asleep,
  Fall asleep, fall asleep,
Suppose the man should fall asleep?
  My fair lady.

Give him a pipe to smoke all night,
  Smoke all night, smoke all night,
Give him a pipe to smoke all night,
  My fair lady.

Hey diddle dinkety, poppety, pet,
The merchants of London they wear scarlet;
Silk in the collar and gold in the hem,
So merrily march the merchant men.

See-saw, sacradown,
Which is the way to London town?
One foot up and the other foot down,
That is the way to London town.

"Oranges and lemons,"
    Say the bells of St. Clements.

"You owe me five farthings,"
    Say the bells of St. Martin's.

"When will you pay me?"
    Say the bells of Old Bailey.

"When I grow rich,"
    Say the bells of Shoreditch.

"When will that be?"
    Say the bells of Stepney.

"I'm sure I don't know,"
    Says the great bell at Bow.

Here comes a candle to light you to bed,
Here comes a chopper to chop off your head.

There was an old woman who lived in a shoe,
She had so many children she didn't know what to do;
She gave them some broth without any bread;
She whipped them all soundly and sent them to bed.

I love little pussy,
    Her coat is so warm,
And if I don't hurt her
    She'll do me no harm.
So I'll not pull her tail,
    Nor drive her away,
But pussy and I
    Very gently will play.

Pussy cat sits beside the fire,
    So pretty and so fair.
In walks the little dog,
    "Ah, Pussy, are you there?
How do you do, Mistress Pussy?
    Mistress Pussy, how do you do?"
"I thank you kindly, little dog,
    I'm very well just now."

Pussy cat, wussicat, with a white foot,
When is your wedding, and I'll come to it.
The beer's to brew, the bread's to bake,
Pussy cat, pussy cat, don't be too late!

Pussy cat Mew jumped over a coal
And in her best petticoat burned a great hole.
Poor pussy's weeping, she'll have no more milk
Until her best petticoat's mended with silk.

Little Robin Redbreast sat upon a tree,
Up went pussy cat, and down went he;
Down came pussy, and away Robin ran;
Says little Robin Redbreast, "Catch me if you can."
Little Robin Redbreast jumped upon a wall,
Pussy cat jumped after him and almost got a fall;
Little Robin chirped and sang, and what did pussy say?
Pussy cat said "Mew" and Robin jumped away.

Great A, little a,
  Bouncing B;
The cat's in the cupboard
  And she can't see.

Ding, dong, bell,
  Pussy's in the well;
Who put her in?
  Little Johnny Green.
Who pulled her out?
  Little Tommy Stout.
What a naughty boy was that,
To try to drown poor pussy cat,
Who never did him any harm,
And killed the mice in his father's barn.

Hey, my kitten, my kitten,
  And hey my kitten, my deary!
Such a sweet pet as this
  There is not far nor neary.
Here we go up, up, up,
  Here we go down, down, downy;
Here we go backwards and forwards,
  And here we go round, round, roundy.

Hoddley, poddley, puddle and fogs,
Cats are to marry the poodle dogs;
Cats in blue jackets and dogs in red hats,
What will become of the mice and the rats?

Puss came dancing out of a barn
With a pair of bagpipes under her arm;
She could sing nothing but "Fiddle-de-dee,
The mouse has married the bumble-bee."
Pipe, cat; dance, mouse;
We'll have a wedding at our good house.

"Pussy cat, pussy cat, where have you been?"
"I've been to London to look at the queen."
"Pussy cat, pussy cat, what did you there?"
"I frightened a little mouse under her chair."

41

This is the key of the kingdom:
In that kingdom is a city,
In that city is a town,
In that town there is a street,
In that street there winds a lane,
In that lane there is a yard,
In that yard there is a house,
In that house there waits a room,
In that room there is a bed,
On that bed there is a basket,
    A basket of flowers.

Flowers in the basket,
Basket on the bed,
Bed in the chamber,
Chamber in the house,
House in the weedy yard,
Yard in the winding lane,
Lane in the broad street,
Street in the high town,
Town in the city,
City in the kingdom:
This is the key of the kingdom.

43

Red sky at night,
Shepherd's delight;
Red sky in the morning,
Shepherd's warning.

A sunshiny shower
Won't last half an hour.

My lady Wind, my lady Wind,
Went round the house to find
    A chink to set her foot in;
She tried the keyhole in the door,
She tried the crevice in the floor,
    And drove the chimney soot in.

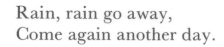

Rain, rain go away,
Come again another day.

As the days grow longer
The storms grow stronger.

When the rain raineth
And the goose winketh,
Little knoweth the gosling
What the goose thinketh.

When the wind is in the East,
'Tis neither good for man nor beast;
When the wind is in the North,
The skilful fisher goes not forth;
When the wind is in the South,
It blows the bait in the fish's mouth;
When the wind is in the West,
Then 'tis at the very best.

March winds and April showers
Bring forth May flowers.

Rain on the green grass,
    And rain on the tree,
Rain on the house-top,
    But not on me.

It's raining, it's pouring,
The old man is snoring,
He went to bed with a cold in the head
And he didn't wake up until morning.

St. Swithin's Day, if thou dost rain,
For forty days it will remain;
St. Swithin's Day, if thou be fine,
For forty days the sun will shine.

Thirty days hath September,
April, June and November;
All the rest have thirty-one,
Excepting February alone,
And that has twenty-eight days clear
And twenty-nine in each leap year.

Mr. East gave a feast;
Mr. North laid the cloth;
Mr. West did his best;
Mr. South burned his mouth
With eating cold potato.

Christmas is coming,
    The geese are getting fat,
Please to put a penny
    In the old man's hat;
If you haven't got a penny,
    A ha'penny will do,
If you haven't got a ha'penny,
    Then God bless you.

Little Jack Horner
Sat in the corner,
Eating a Christmas pie;
He put in his thumb,
And pulled out a plum,
And said, "What a good boy am I!"

I saw three ships come sailing by,
    Come sailing by, come sailing by,
I saw three ships come sailing by,
    On New Year's day in the morning.

And what do you think was in them, then,
    Was in them then, was in them then?
And what do you think was in them then,
    On New Year's day in the morning?

Three pretty girls were in them then,
    Were in them, then, were in them then,
Three pretty girls were in them, then,
    On New Year's day in the morning.

One could whistle, and one could sing,
    And one could play on the violin;
Such joy there was at my wedding,
    On New Year's day in the morning.

"Little Boy Blue,
    Come blow your horn,
The sheep's in the meadow,
    The cow's in the corn;
But where is the boy
    Who looks after the sheep?"
"He's under a haycock,
    Fast asleep."
"Will you wake him?"
    "No, not I,
For if I do,
    He's sure to cry."

What are little boys made of?
What are little boys made of?
   Frogs and snails
    And puppy-dogs' tails,
That's what little boys are made of.

What are little girls made of?
What are little girls made of?
   Sugar and spice
    And all that's nice,
That's what little girls are made of.

The fair maid who, on the first of May,
   Goes to the fields at break of day,
And washes in dew from the hawthorn tree,
   Will ever after handsome be.

Jerry Hall,
He is so small,
A rat could eat him,
Hat and all.

I'm the king of the castle,
Get down you dirty rascal!

Ring-a-ring o' roses,
A pocket full of posies,
  A-tishoo! A-tishoo!
We all fall down.

Here am I,
Little Jumping Joan,
When nobody's with me
I'm all alone.

Moses supposes his toeses are roses,
But Moses supposes erroneously;
For nobody's toeses are posies of roses,
As Moses supposes his toeses to be.

As Tommy Snooks and Bessy Brooks
  Were walking out one Sunday,
Says Tommy Snooks to Bessy Brooks,
  "Tomorrow will be Monday."

There was a little boy and a little girl
　　Lived in an alley;
Says the little boy to the little girl,
　　"Shall I, oh, shall I?"

Says the little girl to the little boy,
　　"What shall we do?"
Says the little boy to the little girl,
　　"I will kiss you!"

Little Miss Muffet
Sat on a tuffet,
Eating her curds and whey;
There came a big spider,
Who sat down beside her
And frightened Miss Muffet away.

Little Blue Ben who lives in the glen,
Keeps a blue cat and one blue hen,
Which lays of blue eggs a score and ten;
Where shall I find little Blue Ben?

　　Go to bed, Tom,
　　Go to bed, Tom.
　　Tired or not,
　　Go to bed, Tom.

　　Jack be nimble,
　　Jack be quick,
　　Jack jump over the candlestick.

Little Polly Flinders
Sat among the cinders,
Warming her pretty little toes;
Her mother came and caught her,
And whipped her little daughter
For spoiling her nice new clothes.

49

Six little mice sat down to spin;
Pussy passed by and she peeped in.
"What are you doing, my little men?"
"Weaving coats for gentlemen."
"Shall I come in and cut off your threads?"
"No, no Mistress Pussy, you'd bite off our heads."
"Oh, no, I'll not; I'll help you to spin."
"That may be so, but you don't come in."

51

Burnie Bee, Burnie Bee,
Tell me when your wedding be?
If it be tomorrow day,
Take your wings and fly away.

Peter Piper picked a peck of pickled pepper;
A peck of pickled pepper Peter Piper picked;
If Peter Piper picked a peck of pickled pepper,
Where's the peck of pickled pepper Peter Piper picked?

Bow, wow, wow,
"Whose dog art thou?"
"Little Tom Tinker's dog."
Bow, wow, wow.

Pit, pat, well-a-day,
Little Robin flew away;
Where can little Robin be?
Gone into the cherry tree.

Come when you're called,
 Do as you're bid,
Shut the door after you,
 Never be chid.

Peter White will ne'er go right;
Would you know the reason why?
He follows his nose wherever he goes,
And that stands all awry.

Up and down the City Road
 In and out the Eagle,
That's the way the money goes,
 Pop goes the weasel.

Half a pound of tuppenny rice,
 Half a pound of treacle,
Mix it up and make it nice,
 Pop goes the weasel!

Every night when I go out,
 The monkey's on the table;
Take a stick and knock it off,
 Pop goes the weasel!

Pretty John Watts,
 We are troubled with rats,
Will you drive them out of the house?
 We have mice, too, in plenty,
 That feast in the pantry;
 But let them stay,
 And nibble away;
What harm is a little brown mouse?

"Is John Smith within?"
"Yes, that he is."
"Can he set a shoe?"
"Aye, marry, two!
 Here a nail and there a nail,
 Tick, tack, too."

There was an old woman
 And nothing she had,
And so this old woman
 Was said to be mad.
She'd nothing to eat,
 She'd nothing to wear,
She'd nothing to lose,
 She'd nothing to fear,
She'd nothing to ask,
 And nothing to give,
And when she did die
 She'd nothing to leave.

Mary had a little lamb,
  Its fleece was white as snow;
And everywhere that Mary went
  The lamb was sure to go.

It followed her to school one day,
  That was against the rule;
It made the children laugh and play
  To see a lamb at school.

And so the teacher turned it out,
  But still it lingered near,
And waited patiently about
  Till Mary did appear.

"Why does the lamb love Mary so?"
  The eager children cry;
"Why, Mary loves the lamb, you know,"
  The teacher did reply.

My mother said, I never should
Play with the gipsies in the wood.
If I did, she would say,
"You naughty girl to disobey.
Your hair shan't curl and your shoes shan't shine,
You gipsy girl, you shan't be mine."
And my father said that if I did
He'd rap my head with the tea-pot lid.

54

Twinkle, twinkle, little star,
How I wonder what you are!
Up above the world so high,
Like a diamond in the sky.

When the blazing sun is gone,
When he nothing shines upon,
Then you show your little light,
Twinkle, twinkle, all the night.

Then the traveller in the dark,
Thanks you for your tiny spark,
He could not see which way to go,
If you did not twinkle so.

In the dark blue sky you keep,
And often through my curtains peep,
For you never shut your eye,
Till the sun is in the sky.

As your bright and tiny spark,
Lights the traveller in the dark,
Though I know not what you are,
Twinkle, twinkle, little star.

"Come, let's to bed,"
    Says Sleepy-head;
"Tarry a while," says Slow;
"Put on the pot,"
    Says Greedy-gut,
"We'll sup before we go."

Rock-a-bye baby,
    Thy cradle is green,
Father's a nobleman,
    Mother's a queen;
And Betty's a lady,
    And wears a gold ring;
And Johnny's a drummer,
    And drums for the king.

Bat, bat, come under my hat,
    And I'll give you a slice of bacon;
And when I bake, I'll give you a cake,
    If I am not mistaken.

"How many miles to Babylon?"
"Three score miles and ten."
"Can I get there by candle-light?"
"Yes, and back again.
    If your heels are nimble and light,
    You may get there by candle-light."

Now I lay me down to sleep,
I pray the Lord my soul to keep;
And if I die before I wake,
I pray the Lord my soul to take.

Cackle, cackle, Mother Goose,
Have you any feathers loose?
Truly have I, pretty fellow,
Half enough to fill a pillow.
Here are quills, take one or two,
And down to make a bed for you.

I see the moon,
    And the moon sees me;
God bless the moon,
    And God bless me.

Rock-a-bye, baby, on the tree top,
When the wind blows, the cradle will rock;
When the bough breaks the cradle will fall,
Down will come baby, cradle, and all.

Go to bed first,
A golden purse;
Go to bed second,
A golden pheasant;
Go to bed third,
A golden bird.

Boys and girls come out to play,
The moon doth shine as bright as day.
Leave your supper and leave your sleep,
And join your playfellows in the street.
Come with a whoop and come with a call,
Come with a good will or not at all.
Up the ladder and down the wall,
A half-penny loaf will serve us all;
You find milk, and I'll find flour,
And we'll have a pudding in half an hour.

Three little ghostesses,
Sitting on postesses,
Eating buttered toastesses,
Greasing their fistesses,
Up to their wristesses,
Oh, what beastesses
To make such feastesses!

Good night,
Sweet repose,
Half the bed,
And all the clothes.

Wee Willie Winkie runs through the town,
Upstairs and downstairs in his night-gown,
Rapping at the window, crying through the lock,
"Are the children all in bed, for now it's eight o'clock?"

The Man in the Moon looked out of the moon,
And this is what he said:
"'Tis time that, now I'm getting up,
All children are in bed."

Friday night's dream
On the Saturday told,
Is sure to come true,
Be it never so old.

The Queen of Hearts
She made some tarts,
All on a summer's day;
The Knave of Hearts
He stole the tarts
And took them clean away.

The King of Hearts
Called for the tarts,
And beat the Knave full sore;
The Knave of Hearts
Brought back the tarts,
And vowed he'd steal no more.

This is the house that Jack built.

This is the malt
That lay in the house that Jack built.

This is the rat,
That ate the malt
That lay in the house that Jack built.

This is the cat,
That killed the rat,
That ate the malt
That lay in the house that Jack built.

This is the dog,
That worried the cat,
That killed the rat,
That ate the malt
That lay in the house that Jack built.

This is the cow with the crumpled horn,
That tossed the dog,
That worried the cat,
That killed the rat,
That ate the malt
That lay in the house that Jack built.

This is the maiden all forlorn,
That milked the cow with the crumpled horn,
That tossed the dog,
That worried the cat,
That killed the rat,
That ate the malt
That lay in the house that Jack built.

This is the man all tattered and torn,
That kissed the maiden all forlorn,
That milked the cow with the crumpled horn,
That tossed the dog,
That worried the cat,
That killed the rat,
That ate the malt
That lay in the house that Jack built.

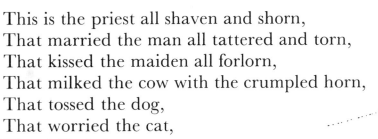

This is the priest all shaven and shorn,
That married the man all tattered and torn,
That kissed the maiden all forlorn,
That milked the cow with the crumpled horn,
That tossed the dog,
That worried the cat,
That killed the rat,
That ate the malt
That lay in the house that Jack built.

This is the cock that crowed in the morn,
That waked the priest all shaven and shorn,
That married the man all tattered and torn,
That kissed the maiden all forlorn,
That milked the cow with the crumpled horn,
That tossed the dog,
That worried the cat,
That killed the rat,
That ate the malt
That lay in the house that Jack built.

This is the farmer sowing his corn,
That kept the cock that crowed in the morn,
That waked the priest all shaven and shorn,
That married the man all tattered and torn,
That kissed the maiden all forlorn,
That milked the cow with the crumpled horn,
That tossed the dog,
That worried the cat,
That killed the rat,
That ate the malt
That lay in the house that Jack built.

If I had a donkey that wouldn't go,
Would I beat him? Oh, no, no!
I'd put him in the barn and give him some corn,
The best little donkey that ever was born.

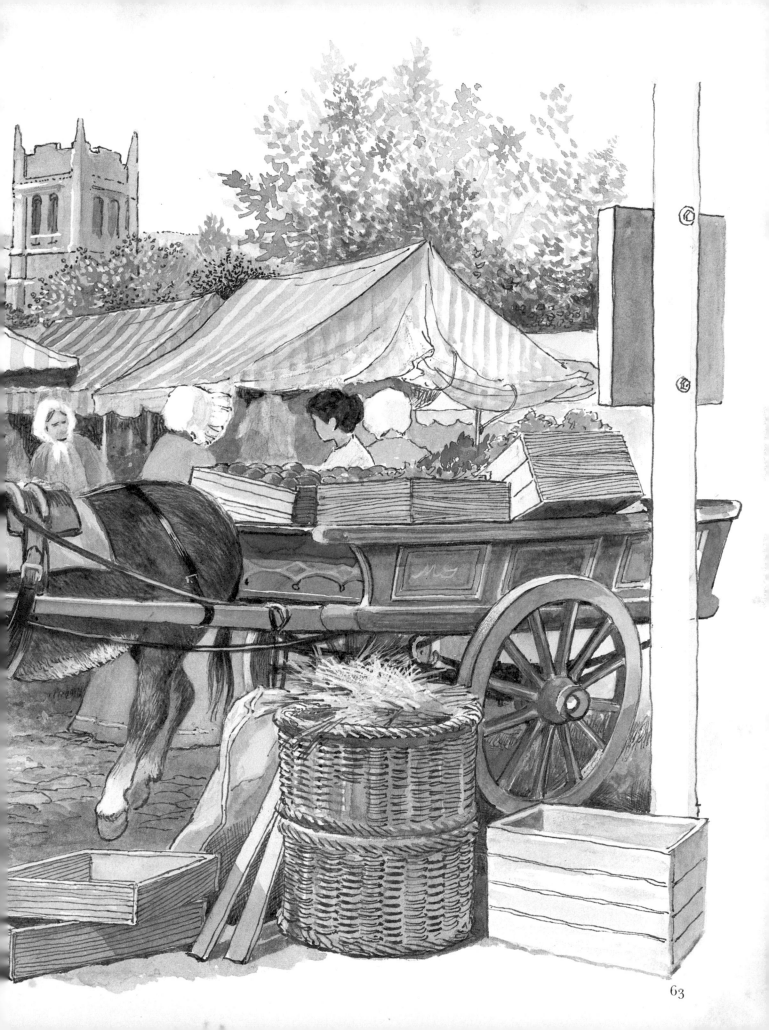

I had a little dog, and his name was Blue Bell,
I gave him some work, and he did it very well;
I sent him upstairs to pick up a pin,
He stepped in the coal-scuttle up to his chin;
I sent him to the garden to pick some sage,
He tumbled down and fell in a rage;
I sent him to the cellar to draw a pot of beer,
He came up again and said there was none there.

   Little Betty Blue
   Lost her holiday shoe;
What can little Betty do?
   Give her another
   To match the other,
And then she may walk out in two.

Here is the church and here is the steeple;
Open the door and here are the people.
Here is the parson going upstairs,
And here he is a-saying his prayers.

There was an old woman sat spinning,
And that's the beginning;
She had a calf,
And that's half;   "Little girl, little girl, where have you been?"
She took it by the tail,   "Gathering roses to give to the Queen."
And threw it over the wall,   "Little girl, little girl, what gave she you?"
And that's all.   "She gave me a diamond as big as my shoe."

A robin and a robin's son   See-saw, Margery Daw,
Once went to town to buy a bun.   Jacky shall have a new master;
They couldn't decide on plum or plain,   Jacky shall have but a penny a day,
And so they went back home again.   Because he can't work any faster.

64

Little Bo-peep has lost her sheep,
　And can't tell where to find them;
Leave them alone, and they'll come home,
　And bring their tails behind them.

Little Bo-peep fell fast asleep,
　And dreamed she heard them bleating;
But when she awoke, she found it a joke,
　For they were still all fleeting.

Then up she took her little crook,
　Determined for to find them;
She found them indeed, but it made her heart bleed,
　For they'd left their tails behind them.

It happened one day, as Bo-peep did stray
　Into a meadow hard by,
There she espied their tails side by side,
　All hung on a tree to dry.

She heaved a sigh, and wiped her eye,
　And over the hillocks went rambling,
And tried what she could, as a shepherdess should,
　To tack again each to its lambkin.

I'll tell you a story
About Jack-a-Nory,
And now my story's begun;
I'll tell you another
Of Jack and his brother,
And now my story is done.

Monday's child is fair of face,

Tuesday's child is full of grace,

Wednesday's child is full of woe,

Thursday's child has far to go,

Friday's child is loving and giving,
Saturday's child works hard for his living,

And the child that is born on the Sabbath day
Is bonny and blithe, and good and gay.

In marble halls as white as milk,
Lined with skin as soft as silk,
Within a fountain crystal clear,
A golden apple doth appear.
No doors there are to this stronghold,
Yet thieves break in and steal the gold.
An egg

I went to the wood and got it;
I sat me down and I sought it;
I kept it still against my will
And so by force home I brought it.
A thorn

A hill full, a hole full,
You cannot catch a bowlful.
Mist

As black as ink and isn't ink,
As white as milk and isn't milk,
As soft as silk and isn't silk,
And hops about like a filly foal.
A magpie

Two legs sat upon three legs
With one leg in his lap;
In comes four legs
And runs away with one leg;
Up jumps two legs,
Catches three legs,
Throws it after four legs,
And makes him bring back one leg.

What God never sees;
What the King seldom sees;
What we see every day;
Read my riddle I pray.
An equal

I have a little sister, they call her Peep-Peep,
She wades the waters, deep, deep, deep;
She climbs the mountains high, high, high;
Poor little creature she has but one eye.
A star

White bird featherless
Flew from Paradise,
Pitched on the castle wall;
Along came Lord Landless,
Took it up handless,
And rode away horseless to the king's white hall.
Snow

Thirty white horses
Upon a red hill,
Now they tramp,
Now they champ,
Now they stand still.
The teeth and gums

Old Mother Twitchett has but one eye,
And a long tail which she can let fly,
And every time she goes over a gap,
She leaves a bit of her tail in a trap.
A needle

Four stiff-standers,
Four dilly-danders,
Two lookers, two crookers,
And a wig-wag.
A cow

As round as an apple,
As deep as a cup,
And all the king's horses
Cannot pull it up.
A well

70

Little King Pippin he built a fine hall,
Pie-crust and pastry-crust that was the wall;
The windows were made of black pudding and white,
And slated with pancakes, you ne'er saw the like.

This little man lived all alone,
And he was a man of sorrow;
For, if the weather was fair today,
He was sure it would rain tomorrow.

My father was a Frenchman,
A Frenchman, a Frenchman,
My father was a Frenchman,
And he bought me a fiddle.
  He cut it here,
  He cut it there,
He cut it through the middle.

Cock-a-doodle-doo!
My dame has lost her shoe,
My master's lost his fiddlestick,
And knows not what to do.

Cock-a-doodle-doo!
What is my dame to do?
Till master finds his fiddlestick,
She'll dance without her shoe.

A diller, a dollar,
A ten-o'clock scholar,
What makes you come so soon?
You used to come at ten o'clock,
But now you come at noon.

The old woman must stand at the tub, tub, tub,
The dirty clothes to rub, rub, rub;
But when they are clean, and fit to be seen,
She'll dress like a lady, and dance on the green.

They that wash on Monday
Have all the week to dry.
They that wash on Tuesday
Are not so much awry.
They that wash on Wednesday
Are not so much to blame.
They that wash on Thursday
Wash for shame.
They that wash on Friday
Wash in need.
And they that wash on Saturday
Oh! They are sluts indeed.

Old Abram Brown is dead and gone,
You'll never see him more.
He used to wear a long, brown coat
That buttoned down before.

Hush thee, my babby,
Lie still with thy daddy,
Thy mammy has gone to the mill,
To grind thee some wheat
To make thee some meat,
Oh, my dear babby, lie still.

Gregory Griggs, Gregory Griggs,
Had twenty-seven different wigs.
He wore them up, he wore them down,
To please the people of the town;
He wore them east, he wore them west,
But he never could tell which he loved
    the best.

Elsie Marley is grown so fine,
She won't get up to feed the swine,
But lies in bed till eight or nine.
    Lazy Elsie Marley.

There was an old woman called Nothing-at-all,
Who lived in a dwelling exceedingly small;
A man stretched his mouth to its utmost extent,
And down at one gulp house and old woman went.

All work and no play makes Jack a dull boy;
All play and no work makes Jack a mere toy.

Tom, Tom, the piper's son,
Stole a pig and away he ran;
    The pig was eat
    And Tom was beat,
And Tom went howling down the street.

Diddle, diddle, dumpling, my son John,
Went to bed with his trousers on;
One shoe off, and one shoe on,
Diddle, diddle, dumpling, my son John.

73

Oh, the grand old Duke of York,
  He had ten thousand men;
He marched them up to the top of the hill,
  And he marched them down again.
And when they were up, they were up,
  And when they were down, they were down,
And when they were only half-way up,
  They were neither up nor down.

74

"Who killed Cock Robin?"
"I," said the Sparrow,
"With my bow and arrow,
  I killed Cock Robin."

"Who saw him die?"
"I," said the Fly,
"With my little eye,
  I saw him die."

"Who caught his blood?"
"I," said the Fish,
"With my little dish,
  I caught his blood."

"Who'll make the shroud?"
"I," said the Beetle,
"With my thread and needle,
  I'll make the shroud."

"Who'll dig his grave?"
"I," said the Owl,
"With my pick and shovel,
  I'll dig his grave."

"Who'll be the parson?"
"I," said the Rook,
"With my little book,
  I'll be the parson."

"Who'll be the clerk?"
"I," said the Lark,
"If it's not in the dark,
  I'll be the clerk."

"Who'll carry the link?"
"I," said the Linnet,
"I'll fetch it in a minute,
  I'll carry the link."

"Who'll be chief mourner?"
"I," said the Dove,
"I mourn for my love,
  I'll be chief mourner."

"Who'll carry the coffin?"
"I," said the Kite,
"If it's not through the night,
  I'll carry the coffin."

"Who'll bear the pall?"
"We," said the Wren,
Both the cock and the hen,
"We'll bear the pall."

"Who'll sing a psalm?"
"I," said the Thrush,
  As she sat on a bush,
"I'll sing a psalm."

"Who'll toll the bell?"
"I," said the Bull,
"Because I can pull,
  I'll toll the bell."

All the birds of the air
Fell a-sighing and a-sobbing,
When they heard the bell toll
For poor Cock Robin.

The winds they did blow,
  The leaves they did wag;
Along came a beggar boy
  And put me in his bag.

He took me up to London,
  A lady did me buy,
Put me in a silver cage,
  And hung me up on high.

With apples by the fire
  And nuts for to crack,
Besides a little feather bed
  To ease my little back.

Oh that I were where I would be,
Then would I be where I am not;
But where I am there I must be,
And where I would be I can not.

I sing, I sing,
From morn till night;
From cares I'm free,
And my heart is light.

Cobbler, cobbler, mend my shoe,
Get it done by half-past two;
Half-past two is much too late,
Get it done by half-past eight.

There was a little boy went into a barn,
   And lay down on some hay;
An owl came out and flew about,
   And the little boy ran away.

Sneeze on Monday, sneeze for danger;
Sneeze on Tuesday, kiss a stranger;
Sneeze on Wednesday, get a letter,
Sneeze on Thursday, something better;
Sneeze on Friday, sneeze for sorrow;
Sneeze on Saturday, joy tomorrow.

Peter, Peter, pumpkin eater,
Had a wife and couldn't keep her;
He put her in a pumpkin shell
And there he kept her very well.

Peter, Peter, pumpkin eater,
Had another, and didn't love her;
Peter learned to read and spell,
And then he loved her very well.

One, two,
Buckle my shoe;
Three, four,
Knock at the door;
Five, six,
Pick up sticks;
Seven, eight,
Lay them straight;
Nine, ten,
A big, fat hen;
Eleven, twelve,
Dig and delve;
Thirteen, fourteen,
Maids a-courting;
Fifteen, sixteen,
Maids in the kitchen;
Seventeen, eighteen,
Maids in waiting;
Nineteen, twenty,
My plate's empty.

Taffy was a Welshman, Taffy was a thief,
Taffy came to my house and stole a piece of beef;
I went to Taffy's house, Taffy wasn't in,
I jumped upon his Sunday hat, and poked it with a pin.

Taffy was a Welshman, Taffy was a sham,
Taffy came to my house and stole a leg of lamb;
I went to Taffy's house, Taffy was away,
I stuffed his socks with sawdust and filled his shoes with clay.

Taffy was a Welshman, Taffy was a cheat,
Taffy came to my house and stole a piece of meat;
I went to Taffy's house, Taffy was not there,
I hung his coat and trousers to roast before a fire.

A swarm of bees in May
Is worth a load of hay;
A swarm of bees in June
Is worth a silver spoon;
A swarm of bees in July
Is not worth a fly.

Bryan O'Lin had no breeches to wear,
So he bought him a sheepskin and made him a pair,
With the skinny side out and the woolly side in,
"Aha, that is warm!" said Bryan O'Lin.

One for sorrow,
Two for joy,
Three for a letter,
Four for a boy,
Five for silver,
Six for gold,
Seven for a secret never to be told.

Oh rare Harry Parry,
When will you marry?
When apples and pears are ripe.
I'll come to your wedding
Without any bidding,
And dance and sing all the night.

This little pig went to market,
This little pig stayed at home,
This little pig had roast beef,
This little pig had none,
And this little pig cried, "Weeee,
    I can't find my way home."

For every evil under the sun,
There is a remedy or there is none.
If there be one, try and find it;
If there be none, never mind it.

There was a jolly miller once,
    Lived on the river Dee;
He worked and sang from morn till night,
    No lark more blithe than he.
And this the burden of his song,
    Forever used to be,
"I care for nobody, no! not I,
    If nobody cares for me."

I had a little nut tree,
   Nothing would it bear
But a silver nutmeg
   And a golden pear.

The King of Spain's daughter
   Came to visit me,
And all for the sake
   Of my little nut tree.

In a cottage in Fife
Lived a man and his wife,
Who, believe me, were comical folk;
For, to people's surprise,
They both saw with their eyes,
And their tongues moved whenever they spoke!
When quite fast asleep,
I've been told that to keep
Their eyes open they could not contrive;
They walked on their feet,
And 'twas thought what they eat
Helped, with drinking, to keep them alive!

I saw a fishpond all on fire
I saw a house bow to a squire
I saw a parson twelve feet high
I saw a cottage near the sky
I saw a balloon made of lead
I saw a coffin drop down dead
I saw two sparrows run a race
I saw two horses making lace
I saw a girl just like a cat
I saw a kitten wear a hat
I saw a man who saw these too
And said though strange,
They all were true.

To market, to market, to buy a fat pig,
Home again, home again, jiggety-jig;
To market, to market, to buy a fat hog,
Home again, home again, jiggety-jog.

We are all in the dumps
For diamonds are trumps;
The kittens are gone to St. Paul's!
The babies are bit,
The moon's in a fit,
And the houses are built without walls.

"Whistle, daughter, whistle,
   And you shall have a sheep."
"Mother I cannot whistle,
   Neither can I sleep."

"Whistle, daughter, whistle,
   And you shall have a cow."
"Mother I cannot whistle,
   Neither know I how."

"Whistle, daughter, whistle,
   And you shall have a man."
"Mother I cannot whistle,
   But I'll do the best I can."

Leg over leg,
   As the fox went to Dover,
When he came to a stile,
   Jump he went over.

The hart he loves the high wood,
   The hare she loves the hill;
The knight he loves his bright sword,
   The lady loves her will.

At Brill on the hill
The wind blows shrill,
The cook no meat can dress;
At Stow-on-the-Wold
The wind blows cold,
I know no more than this.

One misty, moisty morning,
When cloudy was the weather,
There I met an old man
Clothed all in leather;
Clothed all in leather,
With cap under his chin,
How do you do, and how do you do,
And how do you do again?

Ride away, ride away,
   Johnny shall ride,
He shall have a pussy cat
   Tied to one side;
He shall have a little dog
   Tied to the other,
And Johnny shall ride
   To see his grandmother.

Old King Cole
Was a merry old soul
And a merry old soul was he;
He called for his pipe,
And he called for his bowl,
And he called for his fiddlers three.

Every fiddler
Had a fine fiddle
And a very fine fiddle had he;
Oh there's none so rare
As can compare
With King Cole and his fiddlers three.

"What's in there?"
"Gold and money."
"Where's my share?"
"The mousie's run away with it."
"Where's the mousie?"
"In her housie."
"Where's her housie?"
"In the wood."
"Where's the wood?"
"The fire burned it?"
"Where's the fire?"
"The water quenched it."
"Where's the water?"
"The brown bull drank it."
"Where's the brown bull?"
"Behind Burnie's hill."
"Where's Burnie's hill?"
"All dressed in snow."
"Where's the snow?"
"The sun melted it."
"Where's the sun?"
"High, high up in the air."

Round about,
Round about,
Sat a little hare.
The bow-wows came and chased him
Right up there!

Sing, sing, what shall I sing?
The cat's run away with the pudding string!
Do, do, what shall I do?
The cat has bitten it quite in two!

Old Mother Hubbard
Went to the cupboard,
To fetch her poor dog a bone;
But when she got there
The cupboard was bare
And so the poor dog had none.

She went to the baker's
To buy him some bread;
But when she came back
The poor dog was dead.

She went to the undertaker's
To buy him a coffin;
But when she came back
The poor dog was laughing.

She took a clean dish
To get him some tripe;
But when she came back
He was smoking a pipe.

She went to the alehouse
To get him some beer;
But when she came back
The dog sat in a chair.

She went to the tavern
For white wine and red;
But when she came back
The dog stood on his head.

She went to the fruiterer's
To buy him some fruit;
But when she came back
He was playing the flute.

She went to the tailor's
To buy him a coat;
But when she came back
He was riding a goat.

She went to the hatter's
   To buy him a hat;
But when she came back
   He was feeding the cat.

She went to the barber's
   To buy him a wig;
But when she came back
   He was dancing a jig.

She went to the cobbler's
   To buy him some shoes;
But when she came back
   He was reading the news.

She went to the seamstress
   To buy him some linen;
But when she came back
   The dog was a-spinning.

She went to the hosier's
   To buy him some hose;
But when she came back
   He was dressed in his clothes.

The dame made a curtsy,
   The dog made a bow;
The dame said, "Your servant."
   The dog said "Bow-wow."

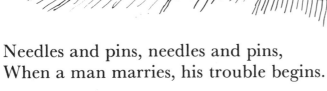

Needles and pins, needles and pins,
When a man marries, his trouble begins.

Here we go round the mulberry bush,
The mulberry bush, the mulberry bush,
Here we go round the mulberry bush,
On a cold and frosty morning.

This is the way we wash our hands
On a cold and frosty morning.

This is the way we wash our clothes
On a cold and frosty morning.

This is the way we go to school
On a cold and frosty morning.

This is the way we come out of school
On a cold and frosty morning.

Hob, shoe, hob,
Hob, shoe, hob,
    Here a nail,
    And there a nail,
And that's well shod.

This is the way the ladies ride,
    Nimble, nimble, nimble, nimble;
This is the way the gentlemen ride,
    A-gallop, a-trot, a-gallop, a-trot;
This is the way the farmers ride,
    Jiggety-jog, jiggety-jog;
And when they come to a hedge – they jump over!
And when they come to a slippery place –
        They scramble, scramble,
        Tumble-down Dick!

"Will you lend me your mare to ride a mile?"
"No, she is lame leaping over a stile."
"Alack! and I must go to the fair,
    I'll give you good money for lending your mare."
"Oh, oh! say you so?
    Money will make the mare to go."

Shoe a little horse,
Shoe a little mare,
But let the little colt
Go bare, bare, bare.

For want of a nail the shoe was lost,
For want of a shoe the horse was lost,
For want of a horse the rider was lost,
For want of a rider the battle was lost,
For want of a battle the kingdom was lost,
And all for the want of a horseshoe nail.

I had a little hobby horse
And it was dapple gray,
Its head was made of pea-straw,
Its tail was made of hay.

I sold him to an old woman
For a copper groat,
And I'll not sing my song again
Without a new coat.

I had a little pony,
    His name was Dapple Gray;
I lent him to a lady
    To ride a mile away.
She whipped him, she slashed him,
    She rode him through the mire;
I would not lend my pony now,
    For all the lady's hire.

Smith, smith, beat them fine,
Can you shoe this horse of mine?
Yes, good sir, that I can,
As well as any other man;
Here a nail, and there a prod,
And now, good sire, your horse is shod.

Rub-a-dub-dub,
Three men in a tub,
And how do you think they got there?
The butcher, the baker,
The candlestick-maker,
They all jumped out of a rotten potato,
'Twas enough to make a man stare.

Little Tee-Wee,
He went to sea,
In an open boat;
And while afloat,
The little boat bended.
My story's ended.

If all the world were paper,
And all the sea were ink,
And all the trees were bread and cheese,
What should we have to drink?

I saw a ship a-sailing,
  A-sailing on the sea,
And oh, but it was laden
  With pretty things for thee.

There were comfits in the cabin,
  And apples in the hold;
The sails were made of silk,
  And the masts were all of gold.

The four-and-twenty sailors,
  That stood between the decks,
Were four-and-twenty white mice
  With chains about their necks.

The captain was a duck
  With a packet on his back,
And when the ship began to move
  The captain said "Quack! Quack!"

Hark, hark
The dogs do bark,
The beggars are coming to town;
Some in rags,
And some in jags,
And one in a velvet gown.

If "ifs" and "ans"
Were pots and pans,
There'd be no need for tinkers.

Ipsey Wipsey spider
  Climbing up the spout;
Down came the rain
  And washed the spider out;
Out came the sunshine
  And dried up all the rain;
Ipsey Wipsey spider
  Climbing up again.

Ladybird, ladybird,
  Fly away home,
Your house is on fire
  And your children all gone;
All except one
  And that's little Ann
And she has crept under
  The warming pan.

Daffy-down-dilly is new come to town,
With a yellow petticoat and a green gown.

As I went over the water,
  The water went over me.
I saw two little blackbirds
  Sitting on a tree;
One called me a rascal,
  And one called me a thief,
I took up my little black stick
  And knocked out all their teeth.

There was an old woman
Who live in Dundee,
And in her back garden
There grew a plum tree;
The plums they grew rotten
Before they grew ripe,
And she sold them for three farthings a pint.

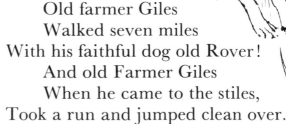

Oh where, oh where has my little dog gone?
  Oh where, oh where can he be?
With his ears cut short and his tail cut long,
  Oh where, oh where is he?

See a pin and pick it up,
All the day you'll have good luck.
See a pin and let it lie,
All the day your luck will fly.

Old farmer Giles
  Walked seven miles
With his faithful dog old Rover!
  And old Farmer Giles
  When he came to the stiles,
Took a run and jumped clean over.

Lucy Locket lost her pocket,
Kitty Fisher found it;
Not a penny was there in it,
Only ribbon round it.

"Jacky come give me thy fiddle,
    If ever you mean to thrive."
"Nay I'll not give my fiddle
    To any man alive.
If I should give my fiddle,
    They'll think that I'm gone mad,
For many a joyful day
    My fiddle and I have had."

"Fire! Fire!" said Mrs. Dyer.
"Where? Where?" said Mrs. Dare.
"Down the town," said Mrs. Brown.
"Any damage?" said Mrs. Gamage.
"None at all," said Mrs. Hall.

There was an old woman
    Lived under a hill,
And if she's not gone
    She lives there still.

Baked apples she sold,
    And cranberry pies,
And she's the old woman
    Who never told lies.

Two little dogs
    Sat by the fire
Over a fender of coal-dust;
    Said one little dog
    To the other little dog,
"If you don't talk, why, I must."

Lavender's blue, diddle, diddle,
    Lavender's green;
When I am king, diddle, diddle,
    You shall be queen.

Call up your men, diddle, diddle,
    Set them to work,
Some to the plough, diddle, diddle,
    Some to the cart.

Some to make hay, diddle, diddle,
    Some to thresh corn,
Whilst you and I, diddle, diddle,
    Keep ourselves warm.

There was a king and he had three daughters,
And they all lived in a basin of water;
    The basin bended,
    My story's ended.
If the basin had been stronger,
My story would have been longer.

Jack and Jill went up the hill
    To fetch a pail of water;
Jack fell down and broke his crown,
    And Jill came tumbling after.

Up Jack got, and home did trot,
    As fast as he could caper,
To old Dame Dob, who patched his nob
    With vinegar and brown paper.

Hey diddle diddle,
The cat and the fiddle,
The cow jumped over the moon;
The little dog laughed
To see such sport,
And the dish ran away with the spoon.

Tommy Trot, a man of law,
Sold his bed and lay on straw;
Sold the straw and slept on grass,
To buy his wife a looking-glass.

In fir tar is,
In oak none is,
In mud eels are,
In clay none are.
Goat eat ivy;
Mare eat oats.

Queen, Queen Caroline,
Washed her hair in turpentine,
Turpentine to make it shine,
Queen, Queen Caroline.

Twelve pairs hanging high,
Twelve knights riding by;
Each knight took a pear,
And yet left a dozen there.

Goosey, goosey gander,
    Whither shall I wander?
Upstairs and downstairs
    And in my lady's chamber.
There I met an old man
    Who would not say his prayers,
I took him by the left leg
    And threw him down the stairs.

If all the seas were one sea,
What a *great* sea that would be!
If all the trees were one tree,
What a *great* tree that would be!
And if all the axes were one axe,
What a *great* axe that would be!
And if all the men were one man,
What a *great* man that would be!
And if the *great* man took the *great* axe,
And cut down the *great* tree,
And let it fall into the *great* sea,
What a splish-splash that would be!

There was a man in our town
And he was wondrous wise,
He jumped into a bramble bush
And scratched out both his eyes;
But when he saw his eyes were out,
With all his might and main,
He jumped into another bush
And scratched them in again.

There was an old woman, and what do you think?
She lived upon nothing but victuals and drink:
Victuals and drink were the chief of her diet,
And yet this old woman could never keep quiet.

She went to the baker to buy her some bread,
And when she came home, her old husband was dead;
She went to the clerk to toll the bell,
And when she came back her old husband was well.

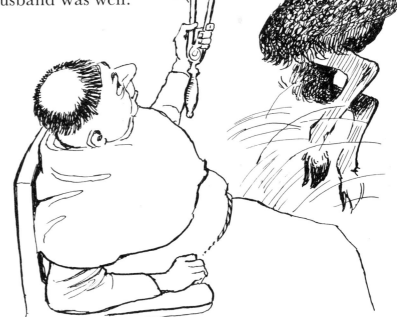

There was a man of double deed
Sowed his garden full of seed.
When the seed began to grow,
'Twas like a garden full of snow;
When the snow began to melt,
'Twas like a ship without a belt;
When the ship began to sail,
'Twas like a bird without a tail;
When the bird began to fly,
'Twas like an eagle in the sky;
When the sky began to roar,
'Twas like a lion at the door;
When the door began to crack,
'Twas like a stick across my back;
When my back began to smart,
'Twas like a penknife in my heart;
When my heart began to bleed,
'Twas death and death and death indeed.

St. Dunstan, as the story goes,
Once pulled the devil by his nose,
With red hot tongs, which made him roar,
That could be heard ten miles or more.

Dickery, dickery, dare,
The pig flew up in the air;
The man in brown soon brought him down,
Dickery, dickery dare.

I had a little husband,
    No bigger than my thumb;
I put him in a pint-pot
    And there I bade him drum.
I bought a little horse
    That galloped up and down;
I bridled him, and saddled him
    And sent him out of town.
I gave him some garters
    To garter up his hose,
And a little silk handkerchief
    To wipe his pretty nose.

As I was going to Banbury,
  Upon a summer's day,
My dame had butter, eggs and fruit,
  And I had corn and hay;
Joe drove the ox, and Tom the swine,
  Dick took the foal and mare,
I sold them all – then home to dine,
  From famous Banbury fair.

As I walked by myself
And talked to myself,
    Myself said unto me,
"Look to thyself,
Take care of thyself,
    For nobody cares for thee.

I answered myself,
And said to myself,
    In the self-same repartee,
"Look to thyself,
Or not to thyself,
    The self-same thing will be."

Cock robin got up early,
    At the break of day,
And went to Jenny's window
    To sing a roundelay.
He sang Cock Robin's love
    To pretty Jenny Wren,
And when he got unto the end,
    Then he began again.

Oh, do you know the muffin man?
    Oh, do you know his name?
Oh, do you know the muffin man
    Who lives in Drury Lane?

Oh, yes, I know the muffin man,
    The muffin man, the muffin man,
Oh yes, I know the muffin man
    Who lives in Drury Lane.

Handy spandy, Jack-a-Dandy,
Loves plum cake and sugar candy;
He bought some at a grocer's shop,
And out he came, hop, hop, hop, hop.

Doctor Foster went to Gloucester
In a shower of rain;
He stepped in a puddle,
Right up to his middle,
And never went there again.

Hickory, dickory, dock,
The mouse ran up the clock.
    The clock struck one,
    The mouse ran down,
Hickory, dickory, dock.

What's the news of the day,
Good neighbour, I pray?
They say the balloon
Is gone up to the moon.

Hot cross buns!
Hot cross buns!
One a penny, two a penny,
Hot cross buns!

If your daughters do not like them
Give them to your sons;
One a penny, two a penny,
Hot cross buns!

I love sixpence, jolly little sixpence,
  I love sixpence better than my life;
I spent a penny of it, I lent a penny of it,
  And I took fourpence home to my wife.

Oh, my little fourpence, jolly little fourpence,
  I love fourpence better than my life;
I spent a penny of it, I lent a penny of it,
  And I took twopence home to my wife.

Oh, my little twopence, jolly little twopence,
  I love twopence better than my life;
I spent a penny of it, I lent a penny of it,
  And I took nothing home to my wife.

Oh my little nothing, jolly little nothing,
  What will nothing buy for my wife?
I have nothing, I spend nothing,
  I love nothing better than my wife.

Barber, barber, shave a pig,
How many hairs will make a wig?
Four and twenty, that's enough.
Give the barber a pinch of snuff.

Charley, Charley,
Stole the barley
Out of the baker's shop.
The baker came out
And gave him a clout,
Which made poor Charley hop.

"Little maid, pretty maid, whither goest thou?"
  "Down in the forest to milk my cow."
"Shall I go with thee?" "No, not now.
  When I send for thee, then come thou."

"Little Bob Robin,
  Where do you live?"
"Up in yonder wood, sir,
  On a hazel twig."

Bye, baby bunting,
Daddy's gone a-hunting,
Gone to get a rabbit skin
To wrap the baby bunting in.

On the first day of Christmas,
My true love sent to me
A partridge in a pear tree.

On the second day of Christmas,
My true love sent to me
Two turtle doves, and
A partridge in a pear tree.

On the third day of Christmas,
My true love sent to me
Three French hens,
Two turtle doves, and
A partridge in a pear tree.

On the fourth day of Christmas,
My true love sent to me
Four colly birds,
Three French hens,
Two turtle doves, and
A partridge in a pear tree.

On the fifth day of Christmas,
My true love sent to me
Five gold rings,
Four colly birds,
Three French hens,
Two turtle doves, and
A partridge in a pear tree.

On the sixth day of Christmas,
My true love sent to me
Six geese a-laying,
Five gold rings,
Four colly birds,
Three French hens,
Two turtle doves, and
A partridge in a pear tree.

On the seventh day of Christmas,
My true love sent to me
Seven swans a-swimming,
Six geese a-laying,
Five gold rings,
Four colly birds,
Three French hens,
Two turtle doves, and
A partridge in a pear tree.

On the eighth day of Christmas,
My true love sent to me
Eight maids a-milking,
Seven swans a-swimming,
Six geese a-laying,
Five gold rings,
Four colly birds,
Three French hens,
Two turtle doves, and
A partridge in a pear tree.

On the ninth day of Christmas,
My true love sent to me
Nine drummers drumming,
Eight maids a-milking,
Seven swans a-swimming,
Six geese a-laying,
Five gold rings,
Four colly birds,
Three French hens,
Two turtle doves, and
A partridge in a pear tree.

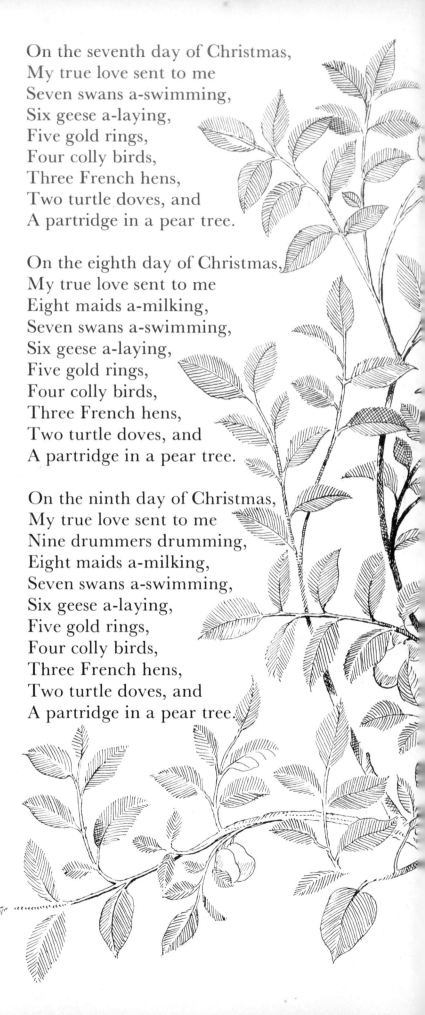

On the tenth day of Christmas,
My true love sent to me
Ten pipers piping,
Nine drummers drumming,
Eight maids a-milking,
Seven swans a-swimming,
Six geese a-laying,
Five gold rings,
Four colly birds,
Three French hens,
Two turtle doves, and
A partridge in a pear tree.

On the eleventh day of Christmas,
My true love sent to me
Eleven ladies dancing,
Ten pipers piping,
Nine drummers drumming,
Eight maids a-milking,
Seven swans a-swimming,
Six geese a-laying,
Five gold rings,
Four colly birds,
Three French hens,
Two turtle doves, and
A partridge in a pear tree.

On the twelfth day of Christmas,
My true love sent to me
Twelve lords a-leaping,
Eleven ladies dancing,
Ten pipers piping,
Nine drummers drumming,
Eight maids a-milking,
Seven swans a-swimming,
Six geese a-laying,
Five gold rings,
Four colly birds,
Three French hens,
Two turtle doves, and
A partridge in a pear tree.

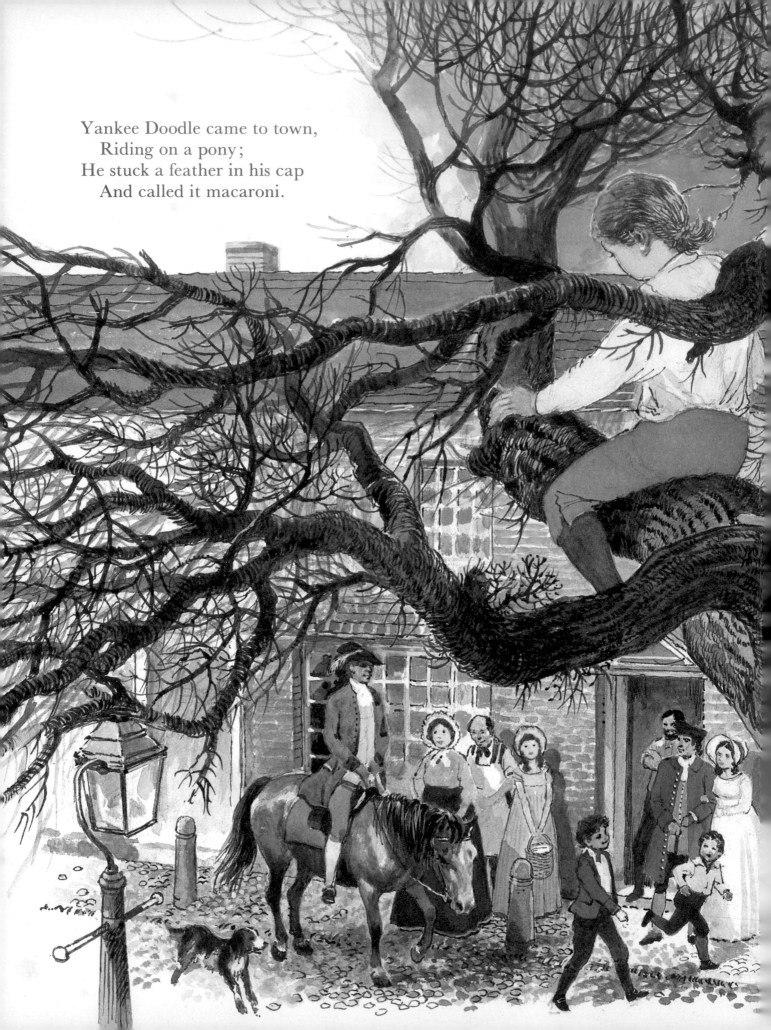

Yankee Doodle came to town,
  Riding on a pony;
He stuck a feather in his cap
  And called it macaroni.

Anna Elise, she jumped with surprise;
The surprise was so quick, it played her a trick;
The trick was so rare, she jumped in a chair;
The chair was so frail, she jumped in a pail;
The pail was so wet, she jumped in a net;
The net was so small, she jumped on the ball;
The ball was so round, she jumped on the ground;
And ever since then she's been turning around.

At the siege of Belle Isle
I was there all the while,
    All the while,
    All the while,
At the siege of Belle Isle.

"Mother may I go and bathe?"
"Yes, my darling daughter.
  Hang your clothes on a hickory limb
  But don't go near the water."

The man in the moon
  Came tumbling down,
And asked the way to Norwich,
  He went by the south
  And burned his mouth
With eating cold pease porridge.

Sally go round the sun,
Sally go round the moon,
Sally go round the chimney pots
On a Sunday afternoon.

There was an old woman tossed up in a basket,
Seventeen times as high as the moon;
Where she was going, I couldn't but ask it,
For in her hand she carried a broom.
"Old woman, old woman, old woman," said I,
"Where are you going to up so high?"
"To brush the cobwebs off the sky!"
"May I go with you?"
"Aye, by and by."

Tinker, tailor,
Soldier, sailor,
Rich man, poor man,
Beggar man, thief.

One, two, three, four, five,
Once I caught a fish alive.
Six, seven, eight, nine, ten,
Then I let it go again.
Why did you let it go?
Because it bit my finger so.
Which finger did it bite?
This little finger on the right.

What is the rhyme for porringer?
What is the rhyme for porringer?
The king he had a daughter fair
And gave the Prince of Orange her.

A man in the wilderness asked me,
"How many strawberries grow in the sea?"
I answered him, as I thought good,
"As many as red herrings grow in the wood."

Snail, snail,
Come out of your hole,
Or else I'll beat you
As black as coal.

Snail, snail,
Put out your horns,
I'll give you bread
And barley corns.

Simple Simon met a pieman,
    Going to the fair;
Says Simple Simon to the pieman,
    "Let me taste your ware."

Says the pieman to Simple Simon,
    "Show me first your penny."
Says Simple Simon to the pieman,
    "Indeed I have not any."

Simple Simon went a-fishing,
    For to catch a whale;
All the water he had got
    Was in his mother's pail.

Simple Simon went to look
    If plums grew on a thistle;
He pricked his finger very much,
    Which made poor Simon whistle.

Matthew, Mark, Luke and John,
Bless the bed that I lie on.
Four corners to my bed,
Four angels round my head:
One to watch and one to pray
And two to bear my soul away.

Index of first lines